ENCHANTAILS™

GRILEGLAS

Lucienne
and the Leopard Boy

Published by Marshall Jones Company
Los Lunas, New Mexico

Based on the characters and universe created by Mark & Tristy Viniello

Library of Congress Control Number: 2015920610

ISBN 978-0-8338-0246-0

ENCHANTAILS: Grileglas Realm Series: Book 1
10-9-8-7-6-5-4-3-2-1
First Edition

Manufactured in the United States of America.

ENCHANTAILS™

Lucienne
and the Leopard Boy

Written by Winter James
Based on characters and universe created by Mark & Tristy Viniello
Illustrations by Alliance Studio
Cover and interior design, additional illustrations by Ken Raney

Marshall Jones Company
Publishers Since 1902
Los Lunas, New Mexico

ILDENOYE

RHOARI

RYUKAI

TIERRA AZUL

ATLANTI

KUMI TAI

GL

CONTENTS

1

My Friend Prince

Her eyes flew open. Princess Lucienne looked over at her bedroom window, a flower carved beautifully into the thick ice of the castle walls. She could see a school of silvery fish swimming by just outside the window. Lucienne enjoyed looking out her window whenever she had a bad dream.

But this wasn't like any of the dreams she had before. This one involved her swimming with some mermaids who turned into sharks and attacked her. She felt goosebumps spread up her arm as she recalled the details of the dream. The chilly water seemed to turn colder.

She needed to forget. Lucienne looked around the room to check if the coast was clear. It was. She swam through the tiny window and out into the open dark waters of the Atlantic Ocean.

Lucienne was never allowed to leave the castle

LUCIENNE

without a guard. Her father would be very disappointed if he discovered she was exploring the icy expanse of her home realm of *Grileglas* alone. She was extra cautious as she swam up to the surface.

She soon broke through a cluster of *ice flowers* that had formulated above her. She found one stuck in her long platinum blonde hair and decided to leave it. She could see a flat iceberg In the distance. It was perfect for star gazing. Lucienne swam over to the giant piece of floating ice and hopped onto it.

Stretched out across the night sky above her was a breathtaking expanse of twinkling stars and galaxies. The scene made her wonder with amazement what it might be like in space. The princess assumed it must be similar to the dark ocean below, full of strange and beautiful things. She pictured herself swimming from planet to planet. She wanted to be anywhere but here.

The other mermaids in her realm did not like Lucienne because she was different from them. They found her strange for loving the surface. They didn't like that she had a guard follow her wherever she went. The mermaids of her realm assumed because she was a princess, Lucienne shouldn't associate with the regular merfolk. They isolated her, no matter how hard she tried to be friends with them.

Lucienne's attention was diverted to a tiny penguin head peering down at her. She sat up and giggled at the penguin walking along the ledge of the glacier behind her.

"*Prince!* What are you doing up there?"

It was her penguin friend Prince, the only friend she had. The penguin looked down at her and began to back up into a run while flapping its tiny wings. The penguin hopped off the ledge into a free fall before Lucienne could react. She was startled, but wiggled her way across the ice to break the penguin's fall. Prince landed in her arms just in time. He looked up at Lucienne with a puzzled look on his face.

"What were you thinking?" Lucienne asked her friend while brushing the snow off its unusual blonde fur. The penguin began squealing and flapping his wings again.

"How many times do I have to tell you, Prince. Penguins can NOT fly," she said, laughing. "I know how you feel, though. I wish I could fly away as well."

Prince is a rare albino Gentoo penguin. He stands out from the crowd because of his constant attempts to fly and his striking blonde hair. Prince often gets left behind by his flock who don't accept him. Lucienne hugged Prince so tightly he let out another squeal.

"Oh, sorry, Prince. It's just that I love you so much!" she exclaimed.

Lucienne remembered the reason she came up to visit the surface. She scratched Prince's belly one more time. She reached back and undid her long blonde hair releasing the tied item holding it

together. Lucienne held the item in front of Prince with a big smile on her face.

"Don't you see, Prince? It's a necklace made just for you. No, it's not just any ordinary necklace, this one was handmade by yours truly."

Prince's eyes widened at the sight of it.

"It's made of pebbles," she told him while wrapping it around his blonde neck.

Prince did a little dance with the pebble necklace bouncing up and down. He loved it. The necklace was made with blue pebbles and sparkled in the moonlight, just like Lucienne's blue tail. It was much too small to be a mermaid necklace, but could easily pass as a hair tie or, better yet, a penguin necklace.

"You look so majestic," she whispered to him kindly. "You already stand out from the crowd, so you might as well stand out even more."

Prince started to run and slide on his belly across the glacier floor. Lucienne laughed and joined him. The two of them slid across the ice until they were both too tired to continue. Lucienne pointed to the different constellations above them as they lay side by side. Her unpleasant dream was almost completely forgotten until a loud roar from behind them sent fear surging through her body again.

2

A Hungry Seal

Lucienne immediately recognized the growl. She wasn't worried for herself though. She was worried for Prince. She turned around and squinted her eyes across the iceberg. She saw a shadow of something large moving in the distance. She knew of only one animal that made that sort of growl. It had to be a *Leopard seal.*

She heard the sound of a different roar as it got closer. But this time it sounded more like the voice of a man, or a boy. Someone was in danger. She needed to help.

"Stay here, Prince! Be still. I'll be right back."

Lucienne mustered all the courage she had and hopped into the water to swim closer to the source of the noise. She put her head up above the surface so only her eyes could be seen, and investigated the scene. The seal was much farther away than she had originally guessed, but it was moving at a fast speed.

The cry she heard earlier changed once again. She hesitated for a moment before swimming closer to the incoming seal. She threw her hand over her mouth to keep herself from making noise.

There was a merman riding the back of the Leopard seal holding a spear. He was howling like an animal. This merman was looking to hunt. He was in no need of help. She didn't waste a moment before dipping back underneath the icy water. She swam as fast as she could back to Prince.

Panic overtook her body and all she could think about was how this might be worse than the nightmare she had earlier. She was back up on the iceberg within seconds grabbing Prince in her arms. They slid at full speed toward an ice tunnel in the glacier. The princess could not let Prince be hunted. She knew she had to find a place to hide him.

The two of them moved quickly through the tiny ice tunnels, sliding down circular chutes that twisted and turned throughout the glacier. Lucienne was so scared she had to close her eyes at one point. She opened them shortly after because the ice tunnel they were going through became so small only Prince could fit. The speed propelled the penguin through the tiny hole as Lucienne got squished in the opening unable to push through.

"Prince!" she screamed, regretting it right after

she heard another growl from the Leopard seal. She didn't know what to do. This was a dead end. She didn't know where Prince was.

Lucienne closed her eyes and felt warmth surge through her hands. She pressed them against the cold tunnel melting the ice in order to create a bigger hole. The seal was now inches away from her, growling and gnashing its sharp teeth. The spotted beast was about to take a bite into Lucienne's neon blue tail before the princess managed to push through the hole into darkness. She looked up as she was falling. She saw the hungry seal attempting to fit through the opening. The seal tried to push his way through, but its body stuck halfway.

Lucienne grinned with relief before splashing into the water at the bottom of the cave. She spotted the pebble necklace she gave Prince earlier glimmering in the distance underneath the surface. She swam over to her poor penguin friend wearing it and hugged him once more. She took him up to the cave floor and laid him down to rest.

"Prince, I want you to stay here until morning. It isn't safe to be wandering right now. That seal is hungry."

The penguin nodded. He seemed to understand what she was saying.

"I need to get back to my realm before my parents wake up and discover I'm missing."

The princess kissed Prince on his head and hopped back into the water. She was extra careful on her way home in case the seal resurfaced. Images of the merman holding a spear filled her mind. Who was he? What was he hunting?

Lucienne thought about alerting her father about this man, but then realized she would be getting herself into trouble by doing so. She also didn't get a good glimpse of the man's face. She certainly wasn't going to be able to sleep after that terrifying encounter.

Merfolk of her realm were strictly warned to stay away from the surface precisely because Leopard seals were so dangerous. Lucienne felt ashamed for disobeying her father. She had put herself and Prince in danger by making a commotion on the glacier.

She silently made her way through the bottom of the iceberg and back into the open waters. Any slight noise or movement scared her enough to make her swim faster. The volcanic ice caves of *Via Solwara* came into view before long. The castle sat in the center of the realm and could be seen from miles away.

The ice towers were tall, narrow and sharp. It was beautiful, but threatening. A lot of dangerous merfolk and creatures passed through these waters, so her people built structures that intimidated intruders. The princess was about halfway through the kingdom before she stopped swimming. She sensed movement coming from behind her.

Could the seal have followed me, she thought, fearful she had put the entire population of Via Solwara in danger. She swam off to the side to take cover behind a jagged cliff. A group of guards passed just beyond the cliff looking for suspicious activity. She would be in major trouble if they discovered her outside of the castle.

The same school of fish Lucienne had seen earlier were passing by again. Now was her chance.

LUCIENNE

She took cover in the center of it, blending in with the fish. The princess watched as the guards completely overlooked the fish and moved on. She stayed in the center of the school until it passed by her window once more just to be safe.

3
The Fall Festival

Lucienne combed her long blonde hair in the mirror, gazing at her reflection. Her pale blue eyes solemnly stared back at her. Lucienne's father had discovered she was leaving late at night to explore the surface and grounded her. The king knew that was the only effective way of punishing her because she hated to be left out of things.

The princess looked down at her royal tiara laying in front of the mirror and picked it up. The tiara was thin and made up of flowers strung together from foreign realms. She smiled at the beauty of the crown and placed it on her head. It was designed to show respect for the other realms.

"Oh that looks beautiful, Adreanna!" said a faint voice outside Lucienne's window.

Lucienne jumped a little at the sound of the familiar voice. She thought at first someone was

talking to her, only to discover the voice came from a group of merfolk gathered outside the castle for the upcoming fall festival.

The princess glanced out the window and gazed down at the mermaids with long, beautiful hair like hers, carving and melting ice sculptures for the big event that would be held the next day. She longed to help them and to take part in the festival.

Groups were huddled around blocks of ice, decorating them and sharing ideas. Lucienne couldn't help but laugh at a group of girls trying to create an ice sculpture of a penguin that ended up looking more like a walrus.

Another group was trying to create a school of fish but kept melting the fins off. Lucienne badly wanted to help them. She was good at this sort of thing. She knew you can't rush when ice sculpting, but not many merfolk knew this.

Many of them were using their whole hand to mold the ice. But the trick was doing little bits at a time by using only one finger. She couldn't sit any longer after several minutes of anxiously watching the merfolk mess up their sculptures. She put the tiara back down and took one last look at herself in the mirror before leaving.

Getting past the guards had become something of a talent for Lucienne. All she had to do was blend in with the regular merfolk. That meant removing her royal sheer cape and putting on something traditional that didn't stand out. She was down in the crowd of festival planners before long.

Lucienne listened as the people, dressed in *aquamarine*, hummed the Grileglas anthem and hastily worked away at their sculptures. Merfolk from throughout the realm would arrive here in the capital city of Via Solwara tomorrow to celebrate her father, *King Izotz*, at castle *Tingim*.

"Can I help you guys?" the undercover princess asked a group of mermaids floating around a block of ice unsure of what to create.

"Yes, please!" said a mermaid with big eyes, "None of us are good at sculpting."

"I have an idea," the princess responded happily.

She immediately began to work at carving out the solar system, complete with every planet and stars in between. It didn't take her very long because she often practiced. Having no friends and being grounded so much gave her plenty of free time. Merfolk began to stop and gather around her praising her work. Almost everyone nearby had come to witness it by the time she had finished. Lucienne hadn't realized how many people were watching. She began to worry about the guards discovering her.

"What is this supposed to be?" said a mermaid with crossed arms floating near Lucienne.

The princess turned around to see who was talking to her. It was a strikingly beautiful mermaid with long, platinum blonde hair. This particular mermaid stood out for her beauty though every mermaid in Grileglas looked alike.

"It's the solar system," replied Lucienne pointing out the different planets, "What's your name?"

"Adreanna," she said with a smirk on her face. "One would have to retreat to the surface to study the sky in order to create the solar system in detail."

Lucienne didn't know how to respond.

"Well, I never would, " she replied with regret.

"Let's hope not," said Adreanna with a hint of sarcasm in her voice. "Who sculpts the skies anyway? We live underwater. Hey everyone, come look at what I've created over here!"

The crowd followed the beautiful mermaid to a tall ice sculpture made in her own image. The crowd showered Adreanna with compliments left and right. Lucienne wondered if they were being genuine or just afraid of Adreanna. She looked back at her own sculpture. No one was left to admire it.

"Maybe Adreanna is right, this sculpture is

terrible," she whispered quietly.

"I think it's beautiful," said a boy swimming up to her from the left.

The boy was paler than most with sandy colored hair and a slightly crooked jaw.

"Thank you," Lucienne responded, surprised. "I like your necklace."

The boy laughed and held it out for her to admire. "It's made of Leopard seal teeth!"

"I don't believe you," she replied grinning.

"Feel it," the boy said, grabbing Lucienne's hand so she could feel the sharpness of the teeth.

The princess pricked her finger on the necklace causing her to jerk her hand back. "But how?" she asked, genuinely curious.

"What's your name?" the boy responded, ignoring her question.

"What's yours?" she asked trying to think of a fake name that wouldn't blow her cover.

The boy laughed.

"Leo," he said holding out his hand to shake. "Just because I ignored your question doesn't mean you can ignore mine."

Adreanna and her friends had returned to break up the conversation before Lucienne could respond. The beautiful mermaid angrily grabbed Leo's arm. "Lucienne doesn't want to be seen talking to a poor leopard boy," she shouted to Leo so everyone around could hear.

"But why?" he responded, removing Adreanna's

hand off of his arm. "How do you know her name?"

Adreanna laughed and pointed at the princess. "Don't you recognize her? That's the princess!"

Leo quickly bowed his head before Lucienne with a shocked look on his face. "Forgive me, princess," he said with remorse.

Lucienne floated back uncomfortably. "No! Don't bow, it's fine. You don't need to apologize. I'm just like you guys."

Adreanna started laughing again. She began shouting to the crowd about the princess being present. "Swim home to daddy. It's not safe out here for a princess," she said sarcastically. "We all know you think you're better than us. You proved it by trying to show off your sculpture."

Lucienne looked around at the many faces, hoping someone would defend her. Nobody did. They began cheering as word got out to the crowd the princess was near them, and surrounded her in hopes of shaking her hand. Lucienne couldn't hold back her tears and began to swim away in a hurry so Leo wouldn't see. The crowd chased her back to the castle where they were stopped by the guards.

4

Thinking About Crystal

The princess sobbed uncontrollably as she swam back into her room. She didn't understand why the people of Grileglas treated her like a caged animal. She was furious at herself for trying to fit in with the mean mermaids and even talking to Leo. She wondered if he agreed with them.

Memories floated back into Lucienne's head of the good old days when her best friend, Crystal, lived nearby. She had short hair and didn't care what others thought of her. Now she was even angrier at herself for crying about this.

She remembered Crystal from long ago, and began missing Prince. Crystal shared her fascination with the land animals and sky. Lucienne had not seen her since Crystal moved to another part of the realm. Crystal still contacted Lucienne occasionally by sending her remnants of things they shared like human treasures and books. Life without her had been lonely. She imagined Crystal telling her to get over this drama and not let Adreanna bother her.

She always reminded Lucienne it was better to stand out than fit in and look like everyone else. Not every mermaid felt the same way Adreanna did, Lucienne thought. She gazed at the human books on her shelf. They were all that was left of her adventures with Crystal.

The memory gave her an idea. She looked around her room for something sharp. She discovered some purple coral In the corner near her mirror given to her as a gift from another realm. The princess took the purple coral and broke a piece off so it became sharp like a blade. She swam in front of the mirror and gathered chunks of her long platinum hair to slice off. She continued to do so until all her hair was cut short like the old days. The coral left the edges of her hair tinted purple. This was a trick Crystal taught her.

She smiled at herself in the mirror, finally remembering who she used to be. She didn't need to impress Adreanna and her friends because she never would. Lucienne giggled. She thought about how all she really wanted was to be was normal like Adreanna, and all Adreanna ever wanted was to be a princess like herself.

Everyone wants what they don't have, she thought, admiring her new cut.

Her mouth dropped at the sight of a head peaking through her window. She quickly turned to find nobody there.

Am I hallucinating? She concluded it was probably just a large fish swimming by. The princess swam over to her dresser to find a boy swimming in the middle of her room.

"AHHH," she screamed, attempting to defend herself with the sharp coral in her hand.

"Whoa, calm down. It's me Leo, remember?"

Lucienne stared at the boy. So many questions were floating in her head. How did he get in? Why was he here? Did he follow her here? What did he think of her hair?

"I... um... what... why... huh?" she muttered.

"Sorry, I didn't mean to scare you," Leo said, laughing. "I thought I'd check up on you since you left in such a hurry."

"Oh, thank you. How did you get past the guards?" she asked while hiding the coral behind her back.

Leo laughed again. "You're not the only one who can evade them," he said quietly. "I like your hair."

Lucienne smiled. "Thank you. I used to wear it like this a long time ago."

"It looks fantastic," he said swimming toward her window again. "I'm sorry for sneaking up on you like that. I just wanted to make sure you were okay. Adreanna can be harsh."

"I learned the hard way," Lucienne said with a grin.

Leo smiled and then stuck his fin out her window, "I'll be going now."

"Wait!" Lucienne shouted. "Where are you going?"

"It's a secret," he whispered.

Lucienne was fascinated with this boy. He was so strange and unique. "I can keep a secret," she whispered.

"Take this," Leo said, pulling out an ice flower from behind his back and blowing it over to Lucienne. It was fresh and beautiful. Lucienne took it in her hands and placed it in her hair once more.

"Wait! How did you get this?" she asked, confused. "They are only found on the surface."

Leo did another one of his mischievous grins and said, "You're not the only one who escapes to the surface." He was gone.

Lucienne gazed out her window still a bit dazed by what just happened. Could she possibly have made a friend other than Prince? She laughed at how ridiculous that sounded. She took the ice flower out of her hair and admired the natural formation. The people of Grileglas were used to seeing the ice flower on garments and letters, but never on themselves. The ice flower was the realm symbol.

She realized something was attached to the flower. It was a note. She ripped it open and read the contents. Leo requested she meet him for an adventure at the ice sculpture of Adreanna in an hour.

Lucienne couldn't contain herself. She wondered what kind of adventure Leo had in store. She swam back and forth in her room looking for the perfect thing to wear. She put on a fancy top with her favorite sea cloak that floated freely behind her. She slipped on her royal bracelet with the aquamarine ice flower in the center. She never left the castle without it.

She waited anxiously until the time came to leave.

5

Follow Me!

Leo was already at the ice version of Adreanna before the princess arrived. He floated in front of the sculpture staring into its eyes.

"Are you having a conversation with Ice Adreanna?" Lucienne asked the leopard boy, scaring him half to death.

"I didn't see you coming," Leo said.

"Now you know how it feels," the princess replied with a giggle.

Leo smiled and complimented her outfit.

"Do you want to know what the ice sculpture of Adreanna and real life Adreanna have in common?" he asked.

"What?"

"They are both cold hearted."

Lucienne laughed and then regretted it. "I think Adreanna just needs some warmth shown to her.

LUCIENNE

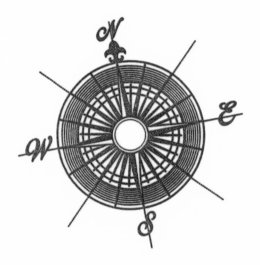

We all do."

Leo nodded and held out his hand.

"Come on. I'm taking you to a place nobody knows about."

Lucienne grabbed his hand even though she was a little hesitant to trust him. Leo had a kindness in his eyes which made her feel more at ease. The boy led Lucienne past multiple homes disguised in the Volcanic ice caves, a few ice plains and a group of mermaids practicing their Sea Dance for the big event tomorrow. They hit a dead end before she knew it.

Leo looked at Lucienne with excitement in his face.

"Here we are!" he said,

The two of them faced a solid ice wall blocking

their path.

"This is your secret?" Lucienne asked, second guessing everything.

"Follow me and do as I do," he told her.

Lucienne agreed, but she was nervous. The boy placed both of his hands on the ice wall in front of him and closed his eyes. She could see the warmth radiate off his pale fingers and onto the wall, melting a hole. The princess helped by placing her hands next to his. they were forming a tunnel through the thick ice before long. A minute passed before they broke through to the other side. Leo couldn't believe how quickly they were moving. Lucienne's power was stronger than he imagined.

"Here we are," he said, grabbing her hand again.

Lucienne squinted her eyes in amazement at what lie in front of them. It was a dark, sandy field covered with what looked like crystal tulips sprouting up from the ground.

"Are they tulips?" Lucienne asked Leo.

"Tulips? What are those?"

"Never mind," she responded with a grin. Lucienne often forgot how little the merfolk know about the land and its plants and animals.

"These are actually animals called *tunicates*," Leo said, pointing to the strange looking organisms. "They are really huge worms that feed on *plankton*."

The princess swam down to the field to examine one closely. The organism planted in the ground was crystal clear and almost glowing.

"Oh, they are beautiful!" The princess said watching them drift in the current. "How did you find this place?"

"I stumbled on it by accident," he responded cheerfully. "I've never taken anybody here before."

Lucienne gazed in amazement at the field of foreign-looking animals. "I feel like I'm in outer space," she said happily.

Leo rarely understood what the princess was talking about. He wasn't sure what outer space meant. He brushed it off and began swimming through the field of organisms at full speed, twisting and turning through the water. Lucienne laughed and followed him. She felt free. Time flew by as they chased each other over the field and explored a nearby cave. She was fascinated with her new friend and his desire for adventure.

"Lucienne! Swim over here," he called out.

She rushed over to Leo who was on the other side of the wall.

"What is it?" Lucienne asked, intrigued.

Leo pointed to a moving creature beneath him, a plump-looking, pink sea creature moving along on the ocean floor with fat little legs. Lucienne laughed.

"It looks like a pig," she cried out. "It's adorable."

Leo was confused again.

"It's an animal that lives on land with the humans," she said in a matter-of-fact tone. "I know a lot about the surface."

Leo swam down to the sea creature and picked it up. "It's a deposit feeder. A *scotoplane*. It eats food by extracting from the mud," he concluded after examining its strange looking mouth tubes.

"It's so plump," Lucienne added, laughing again. "Oh look, there are more."

A whole group of *sea pigs* were approaching from the south. The deep sea never ceased to entertain Lucienne with its many strange creatures that inhabited the realm. The princess and Leo laid on the ocean floor after watching the sea pigs migrate. They gazed up at the sun shimmering through the water.

"Do you see how beautiful this view is?" Leo asked the princess, pointing upward toward the surface.

Lucienne was about to respond but got distracted by something peculiar around Leo's wrist. She sat up to look closer at what was wrapped around it.

"I've seen this before," Lucienne said, grabbing Leo's arm to inspect. A neon blue bracelet made of pebbles was wrapped around his wrist.

"Where did you get this?" Lucienne asked him in a terrified tone.

Leo's eyes widened at Lucienne's sudden change in mood and sat up. He was shocked.

"I…uh…don't remember. It's a long story," he replied, unsure what was making her react the way she did.

Lucienne began to panic. She slowly floated away from the leopard boy. The pebble bracelet Leo was wearing was the necklace she made for Prince. Images of the scary man riding the Leopard seal suddenly flashed into her mind. She couldn't believe what was happening.

"I made that," she whispered. "That shouldn't be here! That should be wrapped around my penguin's neck. What did you do to him?"

Lucienne swam away in a panic before Leo could respond. Prince was in danger. She wondered what Leo did to him. She began to cry, furious at herself for not putting two and two together. She needed to find Prince and make sure he was okay.

LUCIENNE

6

Tell Me Everything

Lucienne entered the castle court wiping tears from her eyes. She had to figure out who the leopard boys were and what they did. She held her head low so the guards wouldn't see her in distress. She passed under the ice arches one by one as the castle servants bowed beside her.

"General!" the princess cried out to an older merman talking to a group of guards outside the chamber entrance. "Is my father in his chamber?"

"Yes, princess, the king is present. Go on in," he said with a quick bow of his head.

Lucienne yanked open the solid doors to the chamber and swam through. She pulled them open so hard she melted the handle. Whenever the princess got heated, her hands did as well.

"Father! Where are you?" she shouted, closing the door behind her.

LUCIENNE

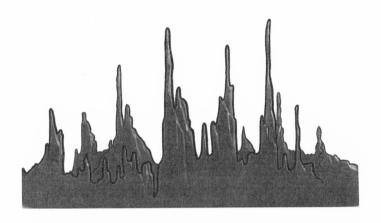

The king's chamber was massive and cold. Its ceiling was almost impossible to see because of its height. The room was perfectly round and took up one of the tall pointy towers that made up the castle. The towers looked like upside down icicles from the outside.

"Lucienne? Is that you?" said a voice from high above her.

Lucienne looked up and saw her father swimming near the top of the room. He was a majestic looking man, with a thick jaw and a long white beard. His power was greater than all the merfolk in the realm, but he was best known for his great wisdom and strength.

"What is troubling you, princess?" King Izotz gently asked his daughter. He sensed something was wrong.

Lucienne's anger faded and sorrow kicked in.

"I'm so sorry, daddy!" she cried.

The king quickly swam up to comfort her. "Tell me everything."

Lucienne held her father close for a few more seconds before letting go. "I disobeyed you again. I left my room and befriended a boy I shouldn't have. I was just so lonely. I needed someone to talk to," she said, as she began crying again at the thought of Prince.

"If only you listened just a little while longer. I was planning to let you enjoy the festival tomorrow."

Lucienne regretted disobeying her father.

The king raised his daughter's chin so he could look into her eyes. "It's a dangerous world outside of these walls," he said calmly. "Every rule and punishment I give is for your own benefit. I want you to be safe. I want you to be happy."

"I realize that now, father," Lucienne replied, angry at herself. "My penguin friend might be dead because of the leopard boys."

The king's face changed. "Leopard boy? Where did you meet a leopard boy?"

"I met him outside the castle. Please tell me who they are."

Her father looked distressed and began swimming in a circle, thinking deeply. His forehead wrinkled up in thought. "This is why I grounded you, Lucienne. To protect you from merfolk like them," the king replied angrily.

LUCIENNE

"Forgive me, father. Who are they?"

The king took a moment before responding and checked outside his chamber door to make sure no one was listening.

"The leopard boys are a group of criminals who race Leopard seals for sport."

The princess looked puzzled. "But why?"

"For money," he said, his voice getting louder with every word. "The leopard boys belong to no realm. They don't follow our laws and practice our customs. The boys are mostly poor orphans, but some are rebellious thrill-seekers. Most were rejected from their hometowns, so they grouped together. Lucienne, this sport is illegal and very dangerous. Many merfolk have lost their lives to the sport over time. We should not interact with Leopard seals. They are incredibly ferocious beasts."

I know that firsthand, she thought.

"Where do these people live?"

"The sport originated in *Ais Solwara* but migrated to the capital," her father told her. "We have been watching them for months. My council has tried to integrate them into society, but they refuse and even rebel. We've had to arrest a handful of them."

Lucienne thought about Leo in the Grileglas jail and felt uncomfortable. "Where do they race?" she asked.

Her father gave Lucienne a stern look. "Why are you asking all these questions?"

LUCIENNE

"Please, father, I need to know."

The king hesitated before answering. "I used to be a leopard boy, Lucienne."

The princess stared at her father. She couldn't believe what she was hearing. The king swam away from her toward the ceiling to collect something hanging from a shelf far above them. He grabbed what looked like a necklace and brought it down to show Lucienne. He held a necklace made of Leopard seal teeth.

"My brother and I joined the leopard boys at an early age," he said with regret. "My brother was killed by a seal."

Lucienne covered her mouth to keep herself from gasping. "I'm so sorry, father," she said. She knew her uncle had died as a child but never knew how.

"Don't apologize," the king responded. "Just understand it is my duty to make sure no merfolk of Grileglas experience the same fate as my brother. I, too, just wanted to fit in with everyone. My brother and I both did."

"So you joined them to escape royal life?" she asked. "But where do the leopard boys race in the capital if it's illegal?"

"Yes. We wanted to be the opposite of royal, and the leopard boys seemed to be free and able to do whatever they wanted. They were everything we were not at the time. We never realized the boys didn't choose the lifestyle. It chose them. They did

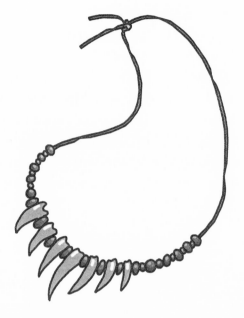

this in order to survive. "They race at the surface and hunt penguins for the seals to eat. They starve the poor seals so they become increasingly hungry and angry and then place the dead penguins at the end of the race to propel the animals to move faster."

Lucienne's heart dropped into her stomach. She began weeping.

"Lucienne, the leopard boys would likely change if the merfolk of Grileglas accepted them for who they are. We rejected them, so they rejected our laws. It is a beautiful quality to stand out from the crowd. That is something you and the leopard boys have in common. You, as the princess, must be an example to the realm of how to treat others.

LUCIENNE

The leopard boys will then appreciate us and stop harming the animals and themselves."

Lucienne hadn't thought about it that way, but still found it hard to forgive anyone who killed innocent penguins.

"You need rest. We both do," her father said trying to comfort her. "You are no longer grounded, I think you've learned your lesson."

Lucienne looked up at her father, bowed her head, and left his chamber.

7

Finding Prince

The princess rubbed another tear from her eye and glanced at herself in the mirror. Her eyes were swollen and her hair was a mess. She wasn't worried about her appearance or what others thought about her. All Lucienne could think about were images of Prince being eaten by a Leopard seal. Her sadness quickly turned to anger. She was free to leave the castle since her father lifted the punishment.

"I'm going to find you, Prince," she muttered.

She decided she either would bring Prince back to safety or give him a proper burial. The thought of burying him made her emotions rise again, so she stopped herself. She had a mission to complete. The princess swam back and forth across her room, collecting items and throwing them into a small bag. She found a small block of ice out in the courtyard and dragged it to her room, after packing the essentials.

Lucienne began melting the edges of the ice block, forming a very large, pointy, ice pick. She needed a weapon to protect herself and figured this would do the job. The tip of the ice pick was so sharp she couldn't even test it without hurting herself. The princess fled her room with her bag and ice pick. She didn't have a moment to spare.

Passing the guards was a lot harder to do with a large weapon but she got out without notice. She made it halfway across the kingdom before realizing her bag had ripped and the food had fallen out. She wondered if the night could get any worse before seeing Leo swim up behind her.

"You dropped these," he said, holding the missing contents of her bag. "I found them floating back there."

Lucienne grabbed the food from Leo's hands and swam away without acknowledging him.

"Are you seriously going to ignore me, princess? I'm not even sure what I've done. You can have

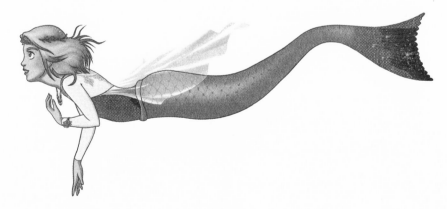

your bracelet!"

Lucienne couldn't stand to listen to the leopard boy any longer.

"It wasn't my bracelet. It belonged to a penguin. A penguin named Prince!" she shouted back at him.

Leo's face turned white. Lucienne continued to shout at the boy, "I made it as a necklace for him. He was so innocent and kind. How could you kill him?"

Leo bowed his head in distress. "Then it's true then," she said. "You are a leopard boy!" "Leave me alone or I'll have you arrested."

Leo followed her anyway. "Your penguin is not dead," he said to her with a little hope in his voice.

This caused Lucienne to stop swimming and face him. "I'm listening."

The boy couldn't look her in the eyes. "I don't remember all the penguins we hunt but I remember this one because it was unusual. Does Prince have blonde fur?"

Lucienne let out a breath of relief. "Yes," she said swimming up to the boy and grabbing his hand.

LUCIENNE

"Where is he?"

"We keep the penguins in a cage near the surface. It's a glacial cavern where we hold the seals and their food."

"Thank you," she said with a little regret about how she treated him. "I have to rescue him."

Leo held onto her hand and wouldn't let go. "Forgive me, princess. I can't let you go alone. You don't know the cavern as well as I do. Let me help."

Lucienne didn't know how to respond. The boy had a look in his eye like he genuinely wanted to help her. She also understood his knowledge of the place would come in handy even if there was a chance he would betray her. She decided to take the risk.

"Leo, listen to me. Animals deserve to be wild and free. They shouldn't be forced to race and penguins shouldn't be hunted by merfolk. We shouldn't interrupt that balance for our own selfish pleasure."

Leo grinned. "I completely agree," he replied. "I'd rather study the plants and animals of Grileglas instead of harming them...."

Lucienne was relieved to hear that.

"Just know I'm not only going to save Prince, I'm going to save all the penguins," she added in case he changed his mind.

"I want to make everything right, too," Leo said getting fired up. "Let's do this!"

Lucienne's face lit up. Leo took her hand and

began swimming as fast he could. They passed by a school of merfolk studying the *glass sponges* in the dark waters.

"I hope you're prepared for a few obstacles," Leo shouted back at her while still moving at a fast speed. "Luckily for us it's late and most of the leopard boys have headed home for the night."

The realization was setting in now about the dangers of the task ahead. She realized not only would they have to deal with hungry seals but also the leopard boys.

"Do not, I repeat, do NOT let anyone know you are the princess," Leo added in a serious tone.

She shuddered at the thought of being caught. Her father had locked up so many of them.

"We can begin ascending to the surface once we reach the outskirts of Via Solwara."

Lucienne closed her eyes and said a silent prayer as Leo lead the way to uncertainty.

LUCIENNE

8

The Coast Was Clear

The two of them traveled slightly farther than usual across the border in case they were spotted. They got behind an ice bluff and took a few moments to rest before ascending. They needed enough energy before swimming up to the surface because, once one makes the trip, there is no stopping for rest.

The princess kept watch as Leo took a few minutes to sleep. She looked back at Leo's face, his eyes closed and his sandy blonde hair floating above him. She was thankful he wanted to help her. She turned around and spotted a whole group of merfolk approaching in the distance.

"Leo, wake up!" Lucienne whispered urgently.

Leo abruptly opened his eyes and swam over to where the princess was floating.

"Who do you think they are?" Lucienne asked.

Leo motioned for her to drop down with him

behind a big nearby rock.

"They don't look like guards," he said, peaking over the rock and squinting his eyes. "I think it's the group of merfolk who were studying the sponges."

"Oh, no," Lucienne said looking down at the rock they were huddled behind. "They are coming to study this rock."

"Huh?" Leo said backing away from the rock. "How do you know?"

"I study more than the stars and the surface," Lucienne said with a grin. "We've already been seen. We need to pretend we're studying this rock too. Let me do all the talking."

Leo nodded his head and before long the group of older merfolk approached the two of them.

"Come to study as well?" an older man asked them with a hint of suspicion.

"Only place we can," Lucienne responded with a laugh, making everyone feel more at ease.

Leo looked out of place with his massive Leopard seal necklace wrapped around his neck. He took it off when no one was looking.

"You've come to the right place, or rock."

Another mermaid cut in. "How long have you been studying?"

"We've actually just finished!" Lucienne replied. "We'll let you guys get to work."

The merfolk seemed kind of surprised the two of them were even studying the rock. Very few

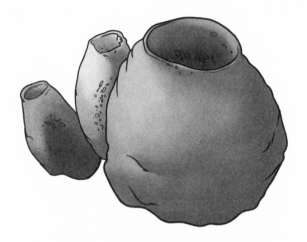

merfolk studied the plants and animals of the
realm. These people held prominent positions and
made lots of money. Lucienne was surprised they
didn't recognize her.

"Good luck!" Leo said with a wave to the
strangers.

The two of them smiled at one another and
swam away from the group of merfolk. They
pretended to swim back into the city but stopped
before entering. The coast was clear before long so
their mission could begin.

Adrenaline kicked in as they sped upward
toward the surface. The water got warmer the
higher they got. The gigantic bottom of an iceberg
came into view halfway along their journey. This
signaled to Leo they were close. Different types
of fish were swimming nearby now that didn't

frequent the city. Leo stopped swimming and turned around to face the princess.

"You'll see a flat surface in the distance once we break the surface. Hop on with me and we'll slide over to another hole in the ice. We'll swim into an underwater ice cavern from there that will take us to the main cave in the center."

Lucienne tried to shake off her nerves. "Let's do this!" she said.

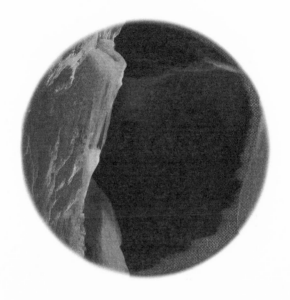

LUCIENNE

9

Swim!

They followed Leo's directions precisely. The hole in the ice was a little farther than Lucienne had expected, but she managed to make it. All those times with Prince taught her how to slide across ice. Lucienne had a hard time keeping up with Leo once they entered the underwater cave. She hardly could see him in the dark.

"It's not much farther," Leo said.

Something long and slimy passed by Lucienne's arm causing her to squirm. The end was in sight. There was a faint glow above them.

"Right now we're in the center of the glacier. The seals should be resting above us, along with the penguin cage and maybe one or two leopard boy guards."

Lucienne could see an orange glow meaning the boys had created fire for light in the cavern. She

assumed they found wood and oil from the massive shipwrecks off the coast.

"You distract the leopard boys while I free the penguins," she whispered.

"Sounds like a plan," Leo said with a wink. "Good luck!"

The cavern was massive. Its ceiling arched high over them with gigantic icicles hanging down above wooden torches frozen into the wall. A tall, cage-like structure made of ice stood in the corner of the cave holding frightened penguins inside. Lucienne counted about 12 Leopard seals sleeping silently across the way. They could hear echoed voices of merfolk having a conversation behind them. They assumed the leopard boys were in the water around the corner of the oddly shaped cave.

Leo motioned for the princess to swim over to

the caged penguins so he could keep watch. She
didn't hesitate. She silently swam over to the cage
careful not to scare the penguins into making a
noise. She listened as the leopard boys around the
corner began laughing. She was glad they were
distracted. The cage sat on an island with water
encircling it.

"This should be easy," she thought.

She swam around the back side peeking her
head above the water. The penguins miraculously
didn't make any noise. Lucienne quickly scanned
the flock looking for her little blonde friend Prince.
He was no where to be found. Butterflies began
filling her stomach in a bad way.

He must be in here, she thought, scanning the
sleeping penguins again. She wondered if Leo had
been lying to her this whole time. She decided not
to second guess him right now. The leopard boys
had stopped laughing, causing her to glance over
and make sure the coast was clear.

Leo gave her a thumbs up.

Lucienne continued to search for Prince when
a noise made her tail twitch. The noise came
from the back of the cage. A tiny blonde penguin
popped its head up from underneath two very large
sleeping penguins.

"Prince!" she whispered.

The penguin let out a squeal of excitement,
flapping its wings back and forth. Lucienne raised
her index finger to her mouth to signal the penguin

LUCIENNE

to be quiet. The penguin didn't understand and was too excited to stop himself. His squeals echoed throughout the cave.

"Quiet!" she whispered, again in a panic.

Prince finally stopped making noise. The cave became eerily silent. The leopard boys were quiet and water droplets could be heard dripping from the ceiling above. Lucienne looked over at Leo again. Something was wrong. She wondered if the leopard boys heard and were suspicious. She was right.

"Hey, guys," Leo said, greeting the two boys approaching him. They were carrying long, dangerous looking weapons.

Lucienne watched as the boys suspiciously interrogated Leo as to why he was here so late. Leo waved his arms around dramatically as he spoke in hopes of distracting them from seeing the princess.

It didn't work. The guards pushed Leo aside and began swimming toward where Lucienne was hiding.

The princess quickly reacted. She melted two of the bars off in front of her and flopped into the center of the penguin cage. Several of the larger penguins angrily snapped at her, but Prince protected her. Lucienne held Prince in her arms and laid in the center. The penguins seemed to sense what was happening and flopped over the princess to protect her from being seen. The leopard boys examined the cage for a moment and then checked the seals nearby for the source of the noise. The seals had slept through the commotion and the boys swam back to Leo.

Lucienne let out a sigh of relief and gave Prince a proper greeting. She never had been so happy to see her best friend.

"I thought you were gone forever," she told him, wiping another tear from her eye. The two of them hugged again. The other penguins began gathering behind them, hopping on top of each other and making noise. She wondered why they were acting so strangely until she heard the growl.

She turned around. A massive Leopard seal was staring at her. She should have known the seals would awake from all this loud noise.

"Swim!" Lucienne shouted to the penguins as the Leopard seal lunged at their cage.

The ice bars shattered in front of her sending

fragments in all directions. She grabbed the ice pick out of her bag to defend herself. The seal attacked her and snapped the weapon in half with its teeth. She smelled the fishy breath of the monster breathing onto her face.

Prince leaped on top of the seals head to distract him. Now was her chance.

The princess hopped out of the cage and led the penguins across the water to the other side of the cavern.

10

A Chance To Fly

Find a way out!" Leo screamed from across the cave.

Lucienne could hear the leopard boys howling in anger. She turned around to find Leo in a fist fight with one of the boys. She wondered where the other one was. All the seals had awakened now, sniffing out the penguins. Some hadn't moved into the water yet, so Lucienne directed her hands towards the ceiling above them and sent out a heat wave.

The warmth melted a crack into the ceiling that dismantled all the massive icicles above them. The icicles fell off the roof one by one onto the ground. Ten seals now were temporarily trapped into a corner. Lucienne bent down to lift a penguin onto the ice just as a spear came flying overhead.

The penguins reacted in a frenzy. Lucienne watched as the other leopard boy hopped onto a

LUCIENNE

seal after throwing his spear. He had a rugged-looking face, bushy eyebrows and long black hair braided behind his back. He looked like he wanted to hunt.

"Prince! Hurry!" She shouted to the penguin attempting to catch up with his flock. The little penguin had confused the first seal so much it got dizzy and knocked itself out. Most of the penguins would have been eaten by now had it not been for Prince.

The leopard boy got control of his seal and directed it towards Lucienne. She had no time to think of a plan so she swam to the corner of the cave with the penguins trailing fast behind her. She looked back and watched as the seal and his rider hopped off the ice and dove into the water. The splash created a wave that rippled over to where they were swimming. Lucienne became uncomfortable at the thought of the boy and his seal swimming beneath them.

She decided to get the penguins to higher ground. Above her was a ledge that cut into the side of the cavern walls. She tried to measure the distance, but couldn't see properly. The water splashing everywhere had put out the torches that lit the cave.

"Prince," she whispered, "remember how you've always wanted to fly?"

The penguin was confused. He thought he already could.

"Now's your chance," she said, a bit nervous about her idea working.

She placed the penguin in the water about a foot away from her tail and kicked up with all the force she could muster. Her tail shot out of the water at full speed, sending Prince high into the air. Lucienne had to laugh at the pure bliss on Prince's face as he flew far above them. He could finally fly.

Lucienne

Gravity soon took over and sent the penguin into a free fall back down onto the ledge.

Lucienne didn't waste a second. She began sending the tiny penguins into the air and onto the ledge one at a time. The final penguin waited his turn and floated in to be kicked. Lucienne kicked up her tail one last time, catapulting the penguin above her. The penguin was mid-air when the seal and his rider came flying out of the water. The seal's mouth was wide open. The penguin bounced off the seal's mouth and flew up toward the others.

"Are you ok?" said Leo, popping out of the water from behind Lucienne.

His hair was matted across his face. His left eye was black and blue.

"Yes, are you? What happened?"

Leo pointed behind him. The leopard boy was swimming toward them at full speed.

"I can't get rid of him!" he said angrily.

"I can't escape the seals!" she shouted back in a panic.

The seals in the corner were now escaping their icicle cage. Leo pointed to a row of whips hanging on the wall beside them.

"They use those to train the seals," he said swimming toward them.

"Throw me one," shouted the princess.

Leo threw a whip over to Lucienne that landed in her hand. The leopard boy jumped out of the water and threw his arms around Lucienne's neck.

"Let her go!" Leo shouted at the leopard boy.

LUCIENNE

Lucienne slipped out of the stronghold and swam beneath and behind her attacker. She took the whip and tied it around the boy's hands. Leo joined her and tied a heavy whip around the attacker's tail so it would drag him down into the depths. They watched as he sunk below unable to swim. The two hugged in excitement.

"We can't swim out from under us. We have to find another way," Leo said, remembering there were still 12 seals after them.

Lucienne grabbed Leo's hands and smiled.

"Do you feel that?" she asked.

Leo removed his hand with a shriek.

"They're hot," he said.

"Exactly! We're going to melt our way out."

11

Time For Dinner

Lucienne dodged another seal as she swam over to the cavern wall. She was determined to get them out of this mess. She wasn't about to give up. Leo and Prince were attempting to distract the seals behind her. Leo hopped onto the ice waving Prince around as bait.

"Time for dinner!" Leo shouted to the hungry seals.

All of the beasts charged after him and the penguin. He waited until the seals were close enough and then dove into a tunnel behind him. The seals crashed into the wall, not able to fit. Lucienne pressed both of her hands against the opposite wall. She closed her eyes to concentrate. Nerves made her hands burning hot. The ice melted so fast she swam through it.

Leo and Prince popped out of another tunnel

nearby and dove into the new one Lucienne had formed. The rest of the penguin flock hopped off the ledge and followed behind. They were out of the cave before long and were sliding across the cold surface of the glacier. The stars lit up the ground much brighter than the torches in the cave had.

"We did it!" Leo shouted in amazement. "I can't believe it."

The group of them let out a cheer. The penguins began happy dancing.

"I think this is yours," Leo said sliding over to Prince who was dancing with his flock that now appreciated him.

He wrapped the pebble necklace around the penguin's neck and smiled.

"I hope you can forgive me, Prince," Leo said kindly. The penguin gave the leopard boy a hug.

A crack in the ice suddenly zigzagged underneath them.

"What's happening?" Lucienne shrieked as another crack shot through the ground beneath her.

Pretty soon the cracks in the ground multiplied and caused the floor to shake.

"The seals!" Leo shouted.

The seals erupted out of the ice from all sides. They were completely surrounded. Multiple leopard boys were now on the backs of the animals.

"Traitor!" shouted one of them, gnashing his teeth at Leo.

Leo held his arms up in front of the princess and the penguins.

"Punish me for this. Let them go!" he shouted back.

Lucienne couldn't allow that. She needed a way out of this. The leopard boy with long braided hair glared at the princess. His mouth fell open.

"That's the princess!" the boy shouted to the others.

An immediate roar came over the crowd. The boys were furious but unsure of what to do.

"Take her hostage!" said one.

"We'll be taken prisoner!" another one shouted.

"It's too late. We've already been seen!"

A few of the Leopard seals grew tired of being held back from the big meal in front of them and began to rebel against their riders. A faint light in the distance caught Lucienne's eye. She recognized something.

"You'll have to get through me first," Leo said with an incredible amount of bravery.

The princess was in awe at his devotion to her. He faced the leopard boys and ripped off his leopard tooth necklace. The boys reacted by spitting on the ice in disgust.

"I'm no longer a part of this!" Leo said as he threw the necklace on the ground.

The boys raised their weapons preparing to fight.

Lucienne knew what she had to do. The Leopard

seals were fearful of nothing, but all merfolk were afraid of one thing: Humans. The princess let out a scream so loud even the seals were frightened. All the little lights in the distance were suddenly directed toward them. Voices could be heard.

"There is a base camp nearby," Lucienne whispered to Leo after her stunning scream. "They are scientists who study Antarctica."

"They heard us," Leo said with worry in his voice.

"That's the point," she told him.

The leopard boy riders looked anxiously behind them as the mysterious figures approached in the distance. Lucienne recognized the sound of the snowmobile the humans used to explore. The engine frightened the leopard boys.

"We need to leave," the boy's leader called out in fury.

All 12 seals and their riders were back beneath the surface within seconds, hidden from view.

"We have to go, too," Lucienne told the penguins. "These people approaching will not hurt you."

Lucienne wondered if they understood, but she didn't have time to explain more.

"I'll be back!" she shouted one last time before disappearing into the water.

Leo took Lucienne's hand and led her back into the realm as quickly as possible. He knew the leopard boys would never show their faces in the capital city due to their identities being revealed. Most would probably retreat to the outskirts or sneak into the trading realm of Atlantis.

Leo was relieved as the shimmering underwater ice castle finally came into view. He was afraid the king might arrest him, but he knew what the leopard boys were doing was wrong. He held his breath as he entered the kingdom

ICE FESTIVAL

The crowds at the Grileglas Ice Festival the next day were huge. Mermaids were dressed in the realm colors with little floral crowns in their hair. Merfolk laughed, cheered, and were enjoying the holiday. Word quickly spread about the disappearance of the leopard boys and people were excited to see the princess and thank her. Rumors about her daring adventure had trickled down through the kingdom overnight.

Lucienne swam into the castle court with Leo by her side. The king approved of Leo because he saved his daughter's life. He had Leo accepted into the only school in Grileglas, where he could study the realm freely. Leo couldn't wait to tell the others the news. The annual ice dance began once the princess and the former leopard boy kicked it off.

The merfolk gasped at the sight of the two of them. Royals never associated with common folk, nonetheless a criminal.

"Thank you for dancing with me," Lucienne whispered to Leo as they swam in circles around the crowd.

"My pleasure," he replied. "You taught me something, princess."

Lucienne blushed. "What could I have possibly taught you?"

Leo looked around at the crowd of shocked faces.

"You taught me not to worry about what others think and to treat everyone equally."

"Including the animals!" Lucienne added with a giggle. "Thank you."

Leo laughed and pointed to the mermaids admiring the princess.

"They cut their hair short like yours," he said.

Lucienne couldn't believe it. All the mermaids around her had cut their hair short to match hers. All except one.

Adreanna angrily watched the happy crowd admire Lucienne and swam off with her long blonde hair flowing behind her.

The rest of the kingdom joined in dancing. Lucienne could not have been happier.

Grileglas Glossary:

1. **Ais Solwara:** the second of the three provinces of Grileglas, which contains the famous "ice graveyard," a bay where many icebergs collect and melt. The famous Ross shelf, the largest ice shelf in Antarctica, is also located here.

2. **Aquamarine:** the realm jewel for Grileglas. It is called the "water of the sea." Aquamarine gems are crystal clear and range from light blue to a deep blue sea color.

3. **Arctic Ice flowers:** the realm symbol for Grileglas, also known "frost flowers." Arctic Ice Flowers form on the surface of the water, when the water vapor particles hit the freezing air, resulting in beautiful sculptures that look like flowers.

4. **Glass Sponge:** large, beautiful, cup-shaped animals that fuse together like a reef in the waters of Antarctica. These "cups" are pale in color, ranging from white to orange, and can grow as large as 6 feet high.

5. **Grileglas:** the name of the Antarctic Realm that Lucienne lives in, which is located in Antarctica in the Southern Ocean.

6. **Izotz:** the King of Grileglas, Lucienne's father.

7. **Leopard Seal:** one of the most ferocious predators in Antarctica, second only to the orca whale. Leopard seals are known by their spotted gray coats. They hunt penguins, and warm blooded prey, including other seals.

8. **Prince:** Lucienne's Sea Buddy. He is an albino Gentoo Penguin, which means his feathers are so light, they are almost white. Gentoo's are usually black and white, recognized by their white stripe that extends like a bonnet over their heads, and their bright orange-red bills. They are the third largest penguins in the world.

9. **Sea Pigs:** fat, pink blobby animals that Lucienne and Leo find, which are actually called "sea cucumbers." They are scavengers with leathery skin and long bodies that feed off the bottom of the sea. They look like little fat pigs.

10 **Sea Worms:** "worms" Leo and Lucienne find that are actually animals called "tunicates." These tube-shaped filter feeders are found on the bottom of the sea in Antarctica. They are clear and look like glass tulips.

11. **Tingim:** the name of the castle of Grileglas.

12. **Via Solwara:** the name of the main province of Grileglas where castle Tingim lies. It is known in Grileglas as the "Volcanic Sea" because of its many hypothermal vents throughout the region.

Lucienne

- Royal Mermaid Daughter of the Grileglas (*pronounced "Grill·ya·gloss"*) Realm
- Name means "light"
- Has short blonde hair with purple ends, electric blue eyes and very pale skin
- Has a shimmering tail of arctic blue
- Special power is heat-manipulation (*the ability to create, shape and manipulate items with heat*)
- Special personality traits are fierce loyalty, bravery, and curiosity that is able to overpower her shyness
- Father is King Izotz (*pronounced "Ee·zot·z"*)
- Home is the Castle Tingim (pronounced *"Teen·gim"*), known for its beautiful ice towers that are tall, narrow and sharp

Prince

- Lucienne's Sea Buddy
- A rare albino Gentoo Penguin who stands 30 inches tall and weighs approx. 12 pounds
- Special ability is speed (*Gentoos are able to swim at a rate of 22 miles an hour, faster than any other diving bird*)
- Wears custom necklace of sea pebbles given to him by Lucienne
- Explores and plays with Lucienne on the glaciers of Antrctica

GRILEGLAS

Mariana Realm

- The Antarctica realm - the coldest realm in the world of Oceana
- Realm symbol is the Arctic ice flower
- Realm colors are ice blue, silver and aquamarine
- Realm jewel is Aquamarine
- Realm motto is "Beauty Within"
- Contains 90 percent of all the ice on the planet
- Is made up of icebergs, sub volcanoes, ice caves, ice deserts and dangerous moving ice forests
- Contains many beautiful, but threatening structures, built to intimidate intruders
- Its first province is called Via Solwara (*pronounced "Vee·ah Saul·war·ah"*) which means "Volcanic Sea" because of its sub volcanoes that are an extension of the mid Atlantic ridge. Via Solwara also contains the dangerous ice forest near the Crozet Islands, and stretches beyond the ice caves of the South Georgia Islands, to the Larsen shelf of the Antarctic Peninsula
- Its second province is called Ais Solwara (*pronounced "Eyes Saul·war·ah"*) which means "Ice Sea," as it includes the ice gardens near Palmer Station and stretches over the giant ice desert to the Bellamy Islands near McMurdo station
- Its third province is called Lait Solwara (*pronounced "Leet Saul·war·ah"*) meaning "Light Sea," which begins near the crab mountains of the Macquarie Ridge, and stretches past the ice islands and whale road off Tasmania to the beautiful ice caves off Enderby Land
- Connects to three other realms: Mahurrab (*pronounced "Ma·hure·ah·b"*) in the Indian Ocean, the Kumi Tai (*pronounced "Coo·me Tie"*) in the Pacific Ocean and Atlantis in the Atlantic Ocean

LUCIENNE
AND PRINCE

LUCIENNE

PRINCE

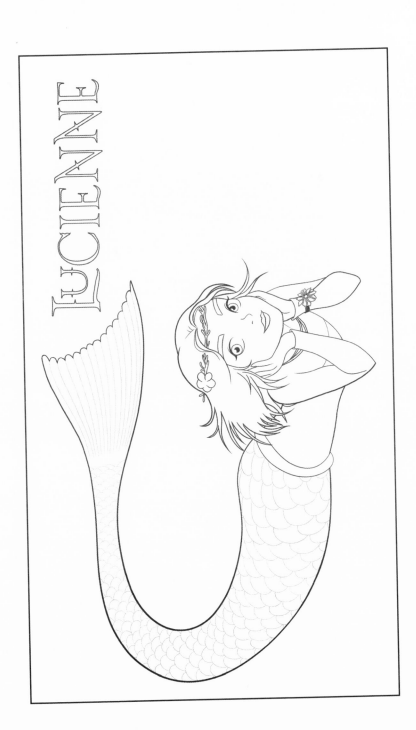

LUCIENNE

More Undersea Adventures...

Smart, outgoing and artistic, Tasi is much more interested in hunting for treasures and creating art with her Sea Buddy, Copper, the tiger tail seahorse, than she is at being a Royal Daughter. But the other merfolk in the Mariana Realm are serious builders and don't understand Tasi's talent. A mermaid named Fan is determined to get Tasi in trouble before she can impress her father, the king. Tasi has a chance to prove her gift is more than just a silly hobby when an explosion of lava threatens the Castle. Will she be able to rally the help she needs in time to save her family from the danger of the deep? Or will Fan succeed in making Tasi look like a fool in front of the entire kingdom?

Visit www.enchantials.com to:

SHOP for more great stories
BUY an Enchantails Slumber Bag Set
LEARN about Oceana's Realms & Royal Mermaid Daughters

Dive Into Other Realms...

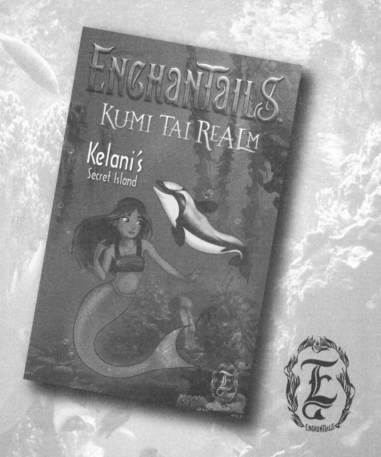

Kelani is a kind, free-spirited royal mermaid who seeks out adventures on her secret island. A deadly adventure interrupts her usual peaceful visit to her hideaway with her Sea Buddy, Keiki an endangered Maui dolphin. Uninvited guests discover her lagoon and begin to destroy the island. Kelani makes an unlikely friendship, and faces her greatest fear in the form of air-breathers (humans). Can Kelani save her island? Can she keep her realm a secret? Or, will the air-breathers ruin her island and expose her world?

Visit www.enchantials.com to:

SHOP for more great stories
BUY an Enchantails Slumber Bag Set
LEARN about Oceana's Realms & Royal Mermaid Daughters